The Witch's Walking Stick

Susan Meddaugh

Houghton Mifflin Company Boston 2005

Walter Lorraine Books

For Kissy

Walter Lorraine Books

Copyright © 2005 by Susan Meddaugh

www.houghtonmifflinbooks.com

Library of Congress Cataloging-in-Publication Data

Meddaugh, Susan.
  The witch's walking stick / by Susan Meddaugh.
      p. cm.
  "Walter Lorraine books."
  Summary: When a witch loses her magic walking stick, which has
been used over the years to grant hundreds of miserable wishes, she
tricks a young girl into finding and returning it, with unexpected
results.
  ISBN 0-618-52948-9
  [1. Witches—Fiction. 2. Wishes—Fiction. 3. Magic—Fiction.] I. Title.
  PZ7.M51273Wiw 2005
  [E]—dc22

                                                          2004017509

ISBN–13: 978-0-618-52948-3

Printed in the United States
WOZ 10 9 8 7 6 5 4 3 2 1

There once was a very old witch who had a magic walking stick. Over the years she had used it to make a thousand miserable wishes come true. It was bent and worn, but it still had just a bit of magic left.

Every day the witch walked through the forest, turning birds into bats or squirrels into goldfish, or doing whatever else she found amusing at the moment.

One day she passed a dog on the path. Shaking her walking stick at the dog, she considered turning him into a cat.

But the dog thought she wanted to play. Before she could make her wish, he grabbed the stick from her hand.

"Give it back!" shrieked the old witch.
Her angry voice so frightened the dog that he ran away with
the stick in his mouth.

"Oh, pickled bats!" groaned the witch. "I'll never catch up
with that dog."

On the other side of the forest, a young girl named Margaret woke up to another bad day.

"Margaret!" yelled her older brother. "Bring me water from the well."

"Margaret!" yelled her older sister. "Sweep the floor and chop some wood."

Selfish, mean, and twice as big as Margaret,
they always got their way.

"Margaret!" they both yelled together. "Make the breakfast.
We want pancakes and we want them now!"

"You wouldn't do this if Mother and Father were still alive,"
cried the girl.

"That's true," they agreed. "Now, don't forget to feed the pigs."

"I think I just did," said Margaret. But not so loud that
they could hear.

Margaret decided then and there to run away.

Unfortunately, she left home without a penny in her pocket. Deep in the woods, she wondered, *How will I survive?*

Margaret followed a path through the woods and soon came upon the witch.
"Girl," moaned the old lady, "a spotted dog has run off with my walking
stick. I can't do a thing without it."
What a sad story, thought Margaret.

"The stick has a star carved on the handle," the witch continued.
"If you can find it and bring it back, I will have a reward for you."
She pulled three shiny gold coins from her pocket.

So Margaret set off to find the dog with the walking stick. *Silly child*, thought the witch. *If you find my magic stick, I will turn you into a mouse and save my coins for another day.*

The spotted dog was not far away.
I wish I had someone to throw this stick for me, he thought.

Not a minute passed before his wish was granted. Margaret came walking along, and the dog dropped the stick at her feet.

But now it was covered with dog drool and bite marks.
"Eeeyew!" said Margaret. "This icky thing can't be the stick
I'm looking for."
So she threw it for the dog.

It was only when the dog brought
it back that she noticed the star
on the handle.

Holding the stick, Margaret said, "I wish I knew why this old piece of wood is worth three gold coins."

And then, having wished it, she knew exactly why.
"A magic stick!" she gasped.
Margaret decided to borrow it for an hour or so.

She went straight home. When she got there, she saw her sister throwing pancakes into the pigpen.
"The pancakes you made for my breakfast got cold," the older girl said, "but I'm sure the pigs will enjoy them."

"I hope you're right," said Margaret. And she turned
her sister into a pig.
"Eat up," she said.

She went into the cottage to find her brother sitting at the table. "Where's my lunch?" he demanded. "I feel like a sandwich today."

"That's funny," said Margaret. "You look like one too."
And she turned her brother into a ham sandwich on rye.

Time for a few more changes, she thought.

Margaret looked at the corner where she slept.

"That's better," she said.

Then Margaret said to her brother and sister,
"The next time you think about being mean to me
remember what happened today."

Still, just to be sure, she silently wished that if they ever forgot,
her brother would have an overwhelming urge to slap mustard
on his head and her sister would start to oink.

Margaret returned her brother and sister to their former shapes.

Then she set out to give the walking stick back to the old lady.

"At last!" croaked the witch when Margaret handed her the stick. "Now, where's that dog? He won't be running away from me ever again!"

She pointed the walking stick toward the dog and said, "You will hang from a hook all summer long, and the only walks you'll get will be when the weather is colder than a witch's heart. For taking my stick, I wish you to be a warm furry doggy HAT!"

Nothing happened.

The witch was puzzled. She looked at the stick.

"You didn't make any wishes with my walking stick, did you?"
she asked Margaret.
"Maybe a few," whispered the girl.

"NOOOOOOO!" howled the witch. "YOU USED UP ALL THE MAGIC! Now it's nothing but a worthless piece of wood!" she cried. And she broke the walking stick against a tree.

Margaret decided it was time to go. As she slipped away, the dog picked up a piece of the stick and followed her.

Back at the cottage, Margaret was happy to find
everything just as she had left it. Even better, in fact.
She fed the dog and threw the stick for him.
"I always wished I had a dog," she told him.